Mem th

by Susan Hartley • illustrated by Anita DuFalla

Mem is a tan hen.
Mem is in the pen.
The pup can see
the hen in the pen.

The pup ran at the pen.
Mem is not in the pen.

The tan hen ran and ran, and the pup ran and ran.

The pup and Mem met Pat.
Pat ran and ran.
The pup and Mem ran and ran.

The hen and the pup met Ben.
"No, pup, no!" said Ben.

Ben has a net.
Mem is in the net.

The hen is in the pen, and the pup is in the hut.